Dragonfall 5 and the Empty Planet

Brian Earnshaw
Illustrated by Simon Stern

Lothrop, Lee & Shepard Company
A Division of William Morrow & Co., Inc.
New York

By Brian Earnshaw

Dragonfall 5 and the Space Cowboys
Dragonfall 5 and the Royal Beast
Dragonfall 5 and the Empty Planet

Published in the United States in 1976. Text copyright © 1973 by
Brian Earnshaw. Illustrations copyright © 1973 by Methuen Children's
Books Ltd. Published in Great Britain in 1973.

Library of Congress Cataloging in Publication Data

Earnshaw, Brian.
  Dragonfall 5 and the empty planet.

  SUMMARY: When their classmates disappear from the circle of singing
stones on the Empty Planet, Tim and Sanchez try to solve the mystery.
  [1. Science fiction] I. Stern, Simon (date) II. Title.
PZ7.E1267Dr4   [Fic]   75-37945
ISBN 0-688-41732-9
ISBN 0-688-51732-3 lib. bdg.

Contents

1. Harvey Allen Galactic High School

"I don't care which school you choose," declared Big Mother, sitting back firmly in the couch at the back of the starship's cabin, "but you must go to one of them for the next four weeks. Four weeks are far too good a chance to miss."

"Four weeks!" wailed Tim and Sanchez together.

"But Big Mother," said Tim, "we haven't been away from *Dragonfall 5* for that long in the last four years!"

"What will happen to Jerk," protested Sanchez, running his hand through the long silky fur of their Flying Hound Dog, "and the Minims?" He nodded up to where the six gray animals sat like chipmunks with pouchy throats on a perch slung from the cabin ceiling.

"Jerk likes anyone who'll feed him," replied Big Mother unkindly, "and we'll be needing the Minims more than ever in the next four weeks; we'll be calling at three different planets, all three speaking different languages. Where we'd be without the Minims I don't know."

The Minims stirred on their perch. Their little beady black eyes looked smugly down and they chattered to one another quietly. They loved to be praised and complimented. It was quite true, too; they were very valuable. They were telepathic and could read every creature's mind that they met. As a result they could speak all the known languages of the universe except those of a few fish people whose noises they could not imitate.

"And how will you manage with the star drive?" asked Tim, who loved machinery. "You know the galactic integrators just aren't working together these days. We came out of star drive a clear hundred thousand miles too soon this time. Look," he said, glaring through one of the ports, "the Empty Planet is only just coming up into circling distance now, and we dropped star drive at least an hour ago."

"What's an hour here and there, boy, when we've got the whole universe to drive around in?" Old Elias, their father, spoke from the controls. Old Elias was usually a little grumpy, but just now he was in a good mood because they were using their rocket pods for the last slow stages of landing. He loved the swoop and thrust of rocket motors. They were doing about eighty thousand miles an hour and they had not reached the Empty Planet's atmosphere yet, so they were having a beautifully smooth ride.

"Look at it there," he waved ahead where the green ball of the Empty Planet swung below them, marked by the clear white patches of hydrogen ice in its upper atmosphere. "There you are," Old Elias continued cheerfully, "safest, quietest, most healthful planet in the known universe. Wish I'd been able to pick up my schooling in a place like that. Clear fresh air and nothing to disturb you."

"Dullest, boringest planet in the known universe," said Sanchez crossly. "No winds, no people, and hardly any animals. And all those dangerous plants and trees rampaging about!"

"Plants down there never hurt anyone that never hurt them," snapped Old Elias. "Besides which, boys," he continued more seriously, "you'll never get your pilot's licenses without certificates to say you've done a course in Star Guidance. If you could show us those certificates in four weeks' time your mother and I would be real proud, wouldn't we, Big Mother?"

"Real proud," said Big Mother shortly. "So you can take your choice, Harvey Allen Galactic High School or the Walking Tree Space Academy, but you'll have to choose fast. We'll be going into landing orbit any minute now and you know what *Dragonfall 5*'s like. She's a good ship but she's an old ship and once these rocket

7

motors have put her into one course they don't take kindly to having to shift her into another. Which is it to be?"

"If we say which one, can we bring *Dragonfall 5* down this time?" asked Tim cunningly. He knew that there was no avoiding school— actually he was looking forward to learning something new—but Old Elias would hardly ever let them take control when they were coming down under rocket power. This looked like a good chance.

"Can they?" asked Big Mother, smiling to herself.

"Which school is it to be?" rapped out Old Elias, tugging grumpily at his white beard.

"Harvey Allen Galactic High School," said Sanchez quickly, because his friend Tanya and her brother Mike were there doing a study of plant life.

"Drat the boys!" declared Old Elias, and wriggled out of the pilot's webbing. "Come on. Take over if you're going to!"

It was a landing to remember for always.

First they had to steer below the Empty Planet's moon. This was a dangerous moon because it was big and could pull spaceships toward it. It was a useless moon, but very beautiful because it was covered in hydrogen ice, and gleamed and flashed like moving water. No one ever went near it.

Then down they circled, heading for the northern half of the Empty Planet where Harvey Allen Galactic High School lay in miles and miles of green rolling downland. Tim fired the retro rockets to slow down their orbit, and Sanchez carefully controlled their sharp orange flames, eyeing them nervously through the ports to see that their trim was just perfect so that Old Elias could not complain.

Dragonfall 5 made one complete circle around the planet with the boys very tense at the controls and th~˙. father muttering to himself as he watc'.ed them.

The Empty Planet had an oxygen atmosphere at ground level, just as Earth has, but at about seven thousand feet up this switched sharply to hydrogen, a very light gas. In this level floated the hard clouds of hydrogen ice which were such a danger to any old-fashioned ship landing on rockets, like *Dragonfall 5*.

The Empty Planet was very calm—winds never blew there—but the clouds of hydrogen ice floated about very slowly, and you were never quite sure where you were going to find them. In these clouds nested the builder birds, who were bigger and much fatter than golden

eagles, and it would have been very bad for *Dragonfall 5* to have bumped into one of those stupid birds. It would have been bad for the birds as well.

"There's an ice cloud eight miles long right plump over Harvey Allen School!" called Sanchez, looking in the scanner which showed a picture of everything a few miles ahead.

"So we can't use the automatic pilot to land," crowed Tim delighted. "Oh, super splendid!"

"Think I'd better take over," said Old Elias anxiously.

"No—let them," said Big Mother, swinging calmly in her hammock couch. "The experience will do them good."

Sharp-nosed and gleaming in black, blue, and silver paint, *Dragonfall 5* rocketed through the bright sunlight toward the tumbled crystal masses of the cloud. Beneath her the ground seemed to mount up toward them.

"Reduce both engines to two point five power," said Tim in a careful quiet voice. *Dragonfall 5* dipped down under the cloud into the lilac green twilight below it. Suddenly the rocket flames seemed brilliant in the dim light. The thunder of the engines echoed tremendously against the ice above them.

"Take her right down onto the school playing field," said Old Elias, far more excited now than any of them. "And see you don't burn a blade of grass or your mother and I will have some explaining to do to the principal!"

"Engines to point five power," said Tim, and then, seconds later, "Engines out!"

The flames and the roar both died, and now, as the school's white buildings showed up a mile ahead through the front port, there was only the gentle rush of air against *Dragonfall 5*'s short curved wings as they soared down.

"Anti-gravs on!" ordered Tim. Sanchez pressed a switch and there was a new humming sound as the great tops began to spin against each other. These anti-gravs did not make *Dragonfall 5* completely weightless but they did make her very much lighter and easier to handle. Now they could see children gathered along one side of the playing fields, all looking up and pointing.

"It's got to be a perfect landing," said Sanchez.

"I know it has," said Tim, and his hands flickered between the anti-grav adjusters and the controls to the flaps of *Dragonfall 5's* swept-back wings. The two schools had been set up on the Empty Planet especially to give an education to the sons and daughters of space pilots, and many of the children at the school were old friends. So if anyone could recognize a bad landing it would be those watching below them.

"Reckon I'll change into my bottle-green dress," said Big Mother, and she walked back to the cabin where they had their living quarters.

This was just like Big Mother, because it was exactly the right thing to do. Suddenly the atmosphere in the control cabin stopped being tense and became casual. Tim did exactly the correct things at exactly the correct time. As they crossed the school boundaries about twenty feet up, he tilted *Dragonfall's* nose ever so gently into a perfect stall and switched the anti-gravs to full power. Buzzing like a great bee, *Dragonfall 5* settled onto her three skid sledges with hardly a bump.

"Made it!" said Sanchez, and scratched Jerk's ear rather hard.

"Not so bad at that," said Old Elias, and lit up his pipe.

Tim said nothing. He just gave Sanchez a look.

Then there was a wonderful moment when

the two boys opened the cabin door and leaned out to greet their friends. They acted very cool and easygoing, as if it were an everyday thing for them to land a starship, but inside they were both bursting with pride as they tipped back their crash helmets and sauntered down the gangway steps.

"Tim! Sanchez!"

"Dropped from heaven!"

"Was it you driving?"

"What are you doing here?"

"How long are you here for?"

It was Mike and Tanya, bursting at them with dozens of questions, Tanya jumping with excitement, Mike much quieter but just as pleased.

Tim and Sanchez grinned at them. Mike and Tanya had been their best friends ever since Old Elias and Mike's father had worked together on the planet Souphrion. But that had been a long time ago and, traveling all over space in *Dragonfall 5*, Tim and Sanchez hadn't seen them for ages. Sanchez was especially pleased to see Tanya. She was as interested in plants and animals as he was, and it would be good to talk to her again. Tim was always much more interested in machinery.

"We're here for four weeks," said Sanchez happily.

"Until we get our Star Guidance certificates," said Tim. "What sort of school is it?"

"Oh, the school's all right," replied Mike with a little suggestion in his voice that something else might not be so good.

"Harvey Allen School's the tops!" burst in Tanya, her eyes bright. "The teachers are really great, even the principal, and they've got the most up-to-date teaching laboratories you ever saw. If you can't get your guidance certificates here you won't get them anywhere. And the plant study gardens, where we do most of our work, are out of this world."

"You can say that again," put in Mike. "We were up this morning at half past five chasing runaway vegetables! We tie them to stakes, and fasten them up in wire cages, and still they get away!"

"Come and see them now," said Tanya. "You've never seen anything like the walking vegetables of Empty Planet. It's the weirdest, nuttiest, most unexpected world we've ever hit. Come on!" and she grabbed both the boys by the arm to pull them toward the school gardens.

"Land sakes, what's your hurry?" It was Big Mother, who had come down the gangway unnoticed. "Your father and I are paying a call on the principal," she said.

15

She had put on her green silk dress with the big emerald clasp instead of the denims she usually wore. Old Elias had put on a green eye shade and combed his hair, but otherwise he was his usual self. The boys were glad about the silk dress. Denims are all very well, but when parents see principals it matters what they wear.

"So don't go far," Big Mother continued. "I've no doubt that the principal will want to see what I'm bringing him," and taking the arm Old Elias had gallantly offered, she sailed grandly across the field toward the school.

"The vegetable pens are near the principal's office," said Tanya, "so we'll go that way and be ready when he calls for you. In any case, morning break is nearly over." They set off after Big Mother and Old Elias, talking busily. As they passed a group of students, however, a blond boy called out, "Hey, Tanya, want to see this weird plant I've trapped?"

"Sorry," said Tanya. "I'm taking Sanchez to see the vegetable pens and we don't have much time."

The boy looked at Sanchez and Tim with a mocking smile.

"Well, hello strangers," he drawled. "Which museum did you steal that old sky bus from?"

"Pay no attention," whispered Tanya urgently. "It's Dave Anderson. He's always like this."

But Dave stepped firmly in front of them, grinning derisively.

"Will it be able to take off again?" he asked, "or shall we tie some builder birds to your tail to help out?"

Tim and Sanchez were furious. *Dragonfall 5* was more than sixty years old, which was very old as starships go, but she had some big advantages over the new fast starships. They loved every rivet in her sleek sides.

"We don't need any help, thank you," said Tim stiffly. "We can take off and land under rocket power anywhere we like. We don't need a special launching cradle to send us off and help us land like the new spaceships you probably travel in."

"Oh, big deal!" sneered Dave. "And how long does it take your creaky old crate to get from here to Earth, three weeks?"

"As a matter of fact," Sanchez rushed in unwisely, "we can get to Earth using our star drive in sixteen days."

"Sixteen days!" roared Dave, and most of the other students laughed with him now. "It takes my father less than five minutes!"

"Come on," whispered Mike. "It's no good arguing with Dave Anderson; he's just a show-off," and the four friends walked away, very red-faced. The trouble was that Dave was right. Modern starships only took a few minutes to pass between a launching platform on one planet and a landing platform on another planet. But they were miserable square boxes, just seats and wire and glass. There was no fun driving them: you just pressed a button, felt giddy for a while, and there you were.

"Never mind," said Tanya. "Even if you have the oldest starship in the universe, it's the best-looking."

And Jerk leaped and whimpered to try to cheer them up because, though he was not a very clever dog, he was very sympathetic.

Tim and Sanchez soon forgot Dave Anderson when Tanya opened a door in a big high wall and showed them the school garden.

At first it was just like an ordinary garden, full of rows of tall beans and fat cabbages and bushes of pale flowers. Then, if you stayed still and watched, you saw that almost all the plants were moving around, pulling their roots from the ground and straining forward. The reason they had to strain was that they were all fastened to stakes in the ground or nails in the wall. The whole garden was like a great green prison.

These were some of the famous walking plants of the Empty Planet. The boys had read all about them, but that was very different from actually seeing them. Fascinated, they walked up and down the restless groves while Tanya and Mike explained how the plants had to be fed certain minerals every day.

"Or they just sulk and die!" Tanya said. "You see that plant on the wall of the principal's office? We call that our rambler rose. It's not a rose at all, but if we didn't tie it down it would ramble right up the wall, over the roof and away!"

"Isn't it rather cruel to keep them penned up?" asked Sanchez, who was very kindhearted.

"It is," said Mike, "but we want to study them, so we never keep any plant here longer than three weeks. We go out once or twice a week in the afternoons to capture new ones to put in their places before we set the old ones free."

"What's that squeaking?" asked Tim suddenly.

"It's Jerk!" said Sanchez anxiously. "Where is he? Something's hurting him!"

"Quick, he's back here!" cried Tanya, and they dashed back down a path to find Jerk crying and terribly upset. A tendril from a plant on

19

one side of the path had caught his nose when he started sniffing it, and a tendril on the other side had caught his tail.

"They're both pulling him," said Sanchez, whipping out his knife.

"No, no, it's all right," laughed Tanya, and she quickly untwisted the plant stems from poor Jerk and patted him. "It's a favorite trick of the plants," she explained, "but they're only being curious; they never hurt."

"This planet is going to take some getting used to," said Sanchez.

"I don't think Jerk will ever get used to it," said Mike, grinning, "Look at him."

Poor Jerk was walking in the very middle of the path, looking nervously on both sides of him and whimpering. Flying Hound Dogs don't have a bark; they can only whimper or howl.

Just then the window of the principal's study flew up,

and Tim and Sanchez were called in to see him.

"See you at lunch," said Tanya. "Don't worry, the principal won't eat you."

She was right. They both liked the principal, who was quite young but rather fat, almost as fat as Big Mother. He was shocked to find how far behind they were in their work, but he promised them a hard four weeks and assigned them to their classes.

"Will they be getting down to work this afternoon?" asked Old Elias, who was still grumpy because he had not landed *Dragonfall 5.*

"No," said the principal. "We get a great deal of knowledge into their heads in the mornings and evenings by using our electric cell infillers and by discussion periods. I insist that they either play games in the afternoon or go out with our field club plant hunting. Games are very important here at Harvey Allen Galactic High School."

"Humph!" said Old Elias, and that was that.

After lunch in the cool white dining room it was time for *Dragonfall 5* to take off. She had been paid to carry some of the mysterious stone statues that are found on the Empty Planet to a museum on Arkel X, a world about two weeks' travel away by *Dragonfall*'s rather slow old star drive.

"I hope you're not taking any of the really beautiful statues with you," said Tanya, as they stood saying goodbye at the gangway. "Some of the Stones we visit on field club outings are wonderful. Not people, you know, just shapes, but you can look at them for ages trying to guess who built them and why."

"*Dragonfall*'s going under her rocket power to a place about six thousand miles away on the other side of this planet. They'll pick the statues up from a site where archaeologists have been digging," explained Tim. "So they won't be taking any that you're fond of."

"Do people really not know who made them?" asked Sanchez. "Surely there must be some clue!"

"Strangely, there isn't," said Mike. "When the first exploring starships got here about twenty years ago the planet was quite empty: just the builder birds in the clouds, and the plants wandering about the ground, and these groups of statues here, there, and everywhere. It was so quiet that everyone said it was the perfect place to build schools in, and that's what they've done."

"And be sure you take advantage of it," said Big Mother firmly. "Goodbye and work hard."

"Be sure you feed Jerk regularly," said Sanchez. "There'll be no danger of our forgetting that dog when he's hungry," said Big Mother, and she winked at Tanya, stepped heavily inside the cabin, and slammed the door.

"Step back!" said Tim. "Old Elias always uses more rocket flame than he needs."

"Listen to the expert," laughed Tanya. But Tim was quite right. The anti-grav tops hummed on and two long yellow flames came thundering out of *Dragonfall 5*'s rocket pods, scorching yards of the playing field. Like a splendid deadly bird she zoomed up, the rocket roar re-echoing from the ice cloud above them, and in seconds she was gone.

23

2. Dave Anderson Tangles the Tapes

"Well, they've only got three of the Minims," said Sanchez, turning to the others. Out of his jacket pocket came three of the little gray animals. They climbed onto his shoulder, where they looked gravely around and then started to tidy their fur.

"You are the limit!" said Tim.

"It's perfectly all right," said Sanchez. "I left a note in the cabin to tell Big Mother where they are. She'll only need the other three Minims to translate for her on Arkel X and I want to see if these three can talk to the walking plants. They'll enjoy a break from being cramped up in *Dragonfall 5*."

"You and your animals," laughed Tim. "Come on—jet polo will be starting in a few minutes. We mustn't be late for games on our very first afternoon."

"I wouldn't mind if I missed games completely," said Sanchez, who hated jet jumpers and jet polo. "I don't think I'm going to like this afternoon."

If you say things like that, afternoons usually

go very badly, and that was what happened that afternoon.

You play jet polo ten to a side. There are no goalkeepers because the goal is only two feet wide. Everyone is mounted on a jet jumper and you keep the ball moving by a blast of air from a hose you hold in one hand. The real skill comes from the way you handle your jumper.

Jet jumpers are not half as smooth and easy as anti-gravs but they are much more fun, if you enjoy machinery. They were very popular at Harvey Allen. Everyone bounced about on brightly painted jumpers like mechanical grasshoppers. Jumpers developed from hovercraft, but they can go up about nine feet in the air and cover six feet in a jump.

Sanchez's team was six goals behind at half time, and a lot of it was Sanchez's fault. Dave Anderson was playing for the other side, and Sanchez was so angry at the way Dave had sneered at *Dragonfall 5* that he lost his temper and played badly whenever Dave came leaping and passing down the right wing, which Sanchez was supposed to be defending.

The real disasters came in the second half. Dave had made a bad squirt with his air hose and let the ball roll much too far ahead of him. It was Sanchez's chance to squirt the ball safely

25

to his own team in mid-field. He pressed his jet button to jump about two yards ahead into squirting position but he pressed much too hard because he was nervous and shot a good five yards over the ball.

"Plunk! Plunk!" Dave's jet jumper came bouncing skillfully down the field with Dave smiling scornfully. Desperately Sanchez pressed again, spinning the control wheel. His jumper and Dave's flew up at exactly the same instant. There was a mid-air collision, a terrific "clang! flop!" of plastic and rubber, and an "Ooo!" from the other boys in the teams.

Sanchez's jumper rolled over on top of him but Dave steadied his jumper in mid-air, landed just by the ball, and squirted a perfect goal to the groans of Sanchez's team.

"Reckon you want a new right-winger," he called to Sanchez's captain. "This one lives in a museum!" and he didn't even get off to see if Sanchez was all right.

It was a very bad afternoon.

Sanchez did not tell the others about his shameful flop in jet polo but they soon found out. Tim was not very pleased because he liked machines, and he was good at jet polo: he had scored three goals in his game. Sanchez could see four miserable weeks ahead with jet polo and misery every afternoon, but Tanya and

26

Mike cheered him up very quickly.

"You don't have to play," Mike assured him.

"You just have to do something to take your mind off work," Tanya butted in. "We're going on a field trip tomorrow afternoon. You can come with us collecting plants for the garden cages."

"Great!" said Sanchez, livening up. "Will we see any of the walking trees I've read about? I've seen walking plants and bushes so far, but no trees."

"Well, we're going to look at the Stones and the statues at Lost Wood Hollow," said Mike. "That's a favorite place for the trees to hang about. You'll be very unlucky if you don't see a few of them."

"But don't count on it," warned Tanya; "they're very temperamental. One day there might be a hundred trees in a valley, all rustling and whispering together, and the next morning none—they've all gone!"

"I'll be happy," promised Sanchez, "so long as I'm not playing jet polo."

"Well, come on," Mike said, "it's time for our evening session under the electric cell infillers."

"Is it painful?" asked Sanchez. "It sounds awful."

"No, it doesn't hurt a bit," Tanya reassured him. "But it does itch!"

They hurried along to the classrooms. Here there were rows and rows of beds, and hanging over the pillows were the electric cell infillers, helmets that looked like the plastic domes of hair dryers.

If you put the helmets on, Mike explained, they send you to sleep and fill your mind with whatever the teachers want to put into them—mathematics, a foreign language, astronomy, anything teachers can think of. Then, when you have had a sleep to digest it, the helmets wake you up with a lively trill of bells and you start a discussion time with the teacher to find out what you have just learned and to make sure you use the information properly. By this method you can compress a year's ordinary work into a few weeks—but, as Tanya said, it does make your head itch.

Each student lay down on a bed, and automatic shutters rolled down over the windows. Where the teacher, Miss Leas, sat there was a bright white light; everywhere else it was dim and green and rather sinister, Sanchez thought as he looked nervously down the row of beds. Dave Anderson was next to him with his eyes shut, but Sanchez didn't think he was really asleep. Tim was lying on the next bed and he gave Sanchez an encouraging wave.

"Right!" called Miss Leas into a microphone

which sounded very deep inside his ear. "Grades three, four, and five in Star Guidance are now going into infiller sleep. But first will you all please check in the little slot at the side of your helmet to see that you have the correct cassette for your course. It wouldn't do for you to learn the wrong course, would it? And mistakes can happen!"

Everyone sat up to check. Sanchez peered carefully at the slot in his helmet. On the cassette which had been slipped into the slot was a label saying 'Star Guidance Course: Grade Three,' so that was all right.

Someone on a bed across the room was in a muddle and Miss Leas walked over to straighten things out. Sanchez lay back looking at the ceiling. It was shadowy and dark and far away, like deep water under low trees. He felt sleepy already.

"Hey, Sanchez," said a voice by his side and he turned in surprise to see Dave Anderson leaning over him.

"Your cassette is almost out of the slot. It's worked loose. You'd have gone to sleep and woken up to find you'd learned nothing. I'll fix it for you."

"Oh thank you, Dave," said Sanchez, feeling

cross because he had bungled machinery again. "Thank you very much."

"Forget it," said Dave. "You're not used to these contraptions, are you?"

He fiddled about with Sanchez's helmet until there was a smart click.

"Now it'll be right," said Dave, and he got back onto his own bed and pulled his infiller down over his head. Tim was looking across at them so Sanchez gave him a thumbs up sign.

"Empty your minds and close your eyes." Miss Leas was speaking into the microphone again. "Infiller sleep is beginning. Trance stage five, four, three, two, one, trance zero."

As her voice grew lower Sanchez felt himself swept away into darkness. Somewhere in the darkness there were pyramids and temples, long bronze trumpets and reed boats toiling up a great brown river. It was not quite what he was expecting, but it looked very interesting. In seconds Sanchez was fast asleep.

Miss Leas looked around at the sleeping class. She had an hour now to get on with her knitting. The heel of the sock which she was turning was quite difficult. She would do it outside on the veranda where there was plenty of light. She went out, pulling the door softly behind her, leaving the electric infillers humming busily in the green light.

But one of the children wasn't listening to his infiller repeating its lesson, because one of the children was wide awake.

It was Tim.

His infiller was chattering gently away about coordinates and prolix angles, but Tim was worried. As trance zero had come he had raised his head out of the helmet and just escaped the electronic sleep. Something was nagging his mind as Miss Leas had counted down. Had there been anything wrong with Sanchez's cas-

sette? It had looked to be perfectly in place. And if there had been anything wrong with it, was it likely that Dave Anderson would be as helpful and smiling as he had been?

It just didn't seem likely.

Cautiously Tim got up from his bed and padded around to Sanchez. Dave Anderson seemed to be fast asleep under his infiller. Tim noticed that Dave was on the same grade of Star Guidance as Sanchez: grade three.

Then Tim bent to check the label on Sanchez's cassette. He peered closely in the green light, then drew a sharp breath.

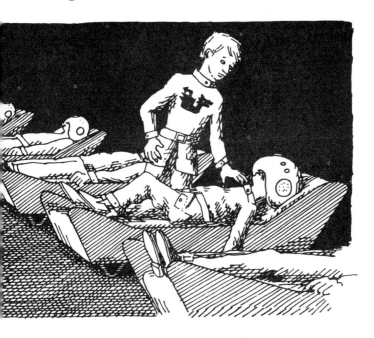

"Wow!" said Tim.

For the label on Sanchez's cassette read quite clearly in gold letters on black:

ANCIENT EGYPTIAN HISTORY
3000 B.C. TO 2000 B.C.

Sanchez was on the wrong course! Dave Anderson had switched cassettes at the last moment.

"What a rotten trick!" Tim whispered to himself.

Tim glanced at the door. There was no sign of Miss Leas. In two swift movements Tim unfixed the cassettes from their sprockets, first from Sanchez's helmet and then from Dave's helmet. Then he reversed them, plugged 'Ancient Egyptian History' into Dave's helmet and 'Star Guidance: Grade Three' into Sanchez's.

The two sleeping boys both mumbled and stirred restlessly. Tim stood frozen between their beds. Silence settled again and he slipped back to his own bed to draw the infiller over his head.

"Ancient Egyptian History!" he thought. "Just wait till they come to the discussion class!"

Smiling, he fell asleep. The electric cell infillers hummed busily away.

An hour later a ripple of bells ran around the room and the shutters purred up from the windows. Miss Leas came in with her knitting and looked at the students as they got sleepily up from their beds, scratching their heads and trying to sort out the new information which was almost part of them.

Dave Anderson smiled cheerfully at Sanchez.

"Feeling all right?" he asked.

"I think so," said Sanchez as he pushed his helmet away.

"You'll be able to guide that museum piece of yours three times around the universe now," said Dave, "blindfold!"

"Yes," said Sanchez. He didn't feel capable of dealing with Dave Anderson just yet. Too many figures were spinning in his mind. He wished that Dave wouldn't grin so much or go on about museum pieces.

"Discussion time!" Miss Leas called brightly. "Grade three make a circle around me, grades four and five gather around Mr. Radmunzen."

Dave Anderson jumped up and began making a circle of beds around Miss Leas, being very polite and helpful all the time.

Sanchez, Tanya, Dave and nine other students gathered around Miss Leas, most of them still hazy and dreamy after their learning sleep. Tim was in a more advanced discussion group with Mr. Radmunzen, a young teacher with spectacles, a tweed coat, and leather-patched sleeves.

"Now," said Miss Leas, "thank you, Dave Anderson, for being so bright and helpful. Good afternoon grade three! Who is going to start us today?"

"I think Sanchez finds it most difficult, Miss Leas," said Dave quickly. "You see, he has been working by himself so he needs most help."

"Why, thank you, Dave," said Miss Leas. "I'm sure you're right. We'll begin with Sanchez."

Sanchez gulped nervously. His mind was a whirl; wasn't there something he should be remembering about pyramids?

"If you were in orbit around Procyon four delta, Sanchez," began Miss Leas crisply, "and you wanted to steer a direct course for the inhabited centers of the Arcturean galaxy, what sightings would you take?"

The group looked expectantly toward Sanchez. Tanya smiled encouragingly, while Dave Anderson gave a wicked grin.

"Why, Miss Leas," said Sanchez, "I'd take a sighting of 0.78 coordinates crossed with 587.662 by 1634 zero, and then I would proceed for roughly fourteen and a half parasecs out of time transit. That should bring me very near to the inhabited sections of Arcturus, probably close to Thorion three beta."

36

"Very, very good," said Miss Leas. "I can see that Sanchez is an excellent learner. Now Dave," she went on, turning to Dave Anderson, who was staring in astonishment at Sanchez after his perfect answer, "perhaps you would tell us what sightings you would take to move from orbit around Thorion three beta back here to the Empty Planet?"

"Uh?" said Dave ungracefully, "what was that?"

Miss Leas repeated her question carefully. A bewildered expression crossed Dave's face and his mouth dropped open.

"Uh!" said Dave, "I don't know what you're talking about Miss Leas."

There was a silence as everyone in the group, and Tim from the next group, stared expectantly at Dave.

"Now, Dave," said Miss Leas sharply, "this isn't like you at all! Wouldn't you sight on an 0.36 coordinate?"

"Uh!" said Dave and looked wildly around the room as if he might see the answer written somewhere.

"And wouldn't you cross it with 2820 point . . . ?" Miss Leas waited hopefully and repeated, "2820."

A sudden understanding crossed Dave's face.

"In 2820 B.C.," he began confidently, "the

fourth dynasty of the Pharaohs, the great kings who built the pyramids, came to an end with the death of the son of Khufu, and the fifth dynasty, a new family of Pharaohs, began to rule much more mildly."

Dave Anderson hesitated and looked around. He stopped smiling. The whole group burst into laughter.

"Dave Anderson!" said Miss Leas crossly, "just which cassette have you been playing in your electric infiller?"

She rose, strode across to Dave's infiller and pulled out the cassette.

"Just what I thought," she said, "Ancient Egyptian History when you should have been studying Star Guidance! What a waste!"

"But, Miss Leas," Dave spluttered, "I don't know how this can have happened." He scowled across at Sanchez.

"I do," Tanya butted in. "Don't you remember, Dave, you got a cassette out of the library this afternoon for private study. You must have got it mixed up with your Star Guidance."

Dave was silent, still glaring suspiciously at Sanchez. Tim in the other group was careful not to catch his eye.

"Well, however it happened," said Miss Leas, "it's all very unfortunate. Dave will have to take a double session on the infiller tomorrow morning to catch up on the Star Guidance he has missed. Which means he will not be playing jet polo tomorrow afternoon because it would be far too much of a mental strain."

"Oh, Miss Leas!" Dave protested.

"Never mind, Dave," Miss Leas smiled encouragingly. "You can come with us on a field trip instead. You'll be able to relax and really unwind, and we'll have no more of these mix-ups between Star Guidance and Ancient Egypt.

"Now the rest of you, back to work! Dave can sit and listen. He'll learn a lot just by listening to Sanchez's answers!"

And that was that. Dave sat and listened in a fuming grump while Sanchez got everything right. Then when discussion was ended Dave stalked off by himself, glowering.

That night Tim told Sanchez what had happened, "Goodness!" said Sanchez, "that's badness rewarded!" and they laughed until the beds shook.

Next morning they were both very careful to check the cassettes of their electric infillers, but there were no more switches. The learning sessions went well for everyone—except poor Dave, who had to have a double session to catch up. This really made his head itch.

Sanchez was very glad when the session was over, even though it had gone well. He was looking forward to the field trip and a chance to see the strange wandering woods of the Empty Planet.

"Are you coming with us, Tim?" he asked as they sat in the dining hall eating cereal crunch and grasshoppers fried in batter.

"You catch me wasting a whole afternoon chasing plants or looking around old ruins!" replied Tim scornfully. "I'm going to play jet polo. Dave Anderson is out of the game and they are trying me in his place in the first team. With any luck I'll be chosen to play against Walking Tree Space Academy next week."

"Old Elias will say you've been playing too many games," said Sanchez. "So you sure will have to get your Star Guidance certificate now to prove that you've done your schoolwork too!"

"My head itches enough after this morning's work," said Tim.

"Mine too! Will Mother and Dad have taken off for Arkel X yet?" asked Sanchez rather sadly. "I miss Jerk. I wish I'd smuggled him out as well as the Minims."

"No, they'll be loading up these statues all today, and they won't blast off until after breakfast tomorrow. But Jerk just wouldn't have fitted into school here. You know how excited he always gets about people."

"I suppose you're right," agreed Sanchez gloomily. They were eating an ice cream roving-fruit pie now, full of delicious berries that tasted like a cross between raspberries and peaches.

"Don't be miserable," went on Tim. "You'll have Dave Anderson to keep you company this afternoon on the field trip!"

This was mean of Tim, but he still felt cross over what Sanchez had said about playing too many games.

"Oh no!" Sanchez wailed, and dug viciously into his roving-fruit pie. He had seen quite enough of Dave Anderson the day before.

3. The Singing Stones

After lunch the students who were going on the field trip to Lost Wood Hollow gathered outside school with their brightly painted plastic jet jumpers. There were about twenty-five of them. Mr. Radmunzen and Miss Leas were in charge; they were busy checking everyone's jet jumpers and seeing that no one had forgotten his snack pack.

Dave Anderson was riding a brilliantly striped black-and-yellow jumper and already he was showing off to Tanya, doing mid-air spins in the middle of a leap.

"Does Dave know Tanya quite well?" Sanchez asked Mike.

"Well," said Mike, "he tries to. I think that's really why he's so rotten to you—because you're her friend."

"Oh!" said Sanchez. "Today isn't going to be any better than yesterday!" He sat nervously on the seat of his old and battered jumper.

At a signal from Mr. Radmunzen they were all off up the green hill slopes. In the stillness of the Empty Planet they made a tremendous noise. Each jumper as it leaps along makes a "clump" sound, like those road graders that flatten road surfaces. So with nearly thirty of them and everyone singing and shouting as well, there was quite a racket.

The turf on the Empty Planet is very deep, like a thick grass sponge, and so bouncy that it is quite difficult to walk on. As the field trip party careered along, the jumpers disturbed whole swarms of little insects and creepy-crawlies that lived in the turf. This soon attracted the builder birds down from their ice clouds high above and they swooped around with their harsh low cries, adding to the din.

Even Sanchez could not help enjoying it, despite his low opinion of jet jumpers. Ten of them played a wild game of leapfrog for three miles or more, leaping and swooshing through the still air, often falling off, but scrambling on again to go on "blop! blop! blop!" up slope and down slope.

The point of the game was to make kings. You made a king by jumping your jet clean over someone else's jet when it was on the ground. Since they were probably busy trying to jump over someone else, it got rather complicated and it was a good thing that the jet jumpers were padded in rubber.

Sanchez collided and fell out four times, but

he didn't mind because he made Dave Anderson fall out once by going up just as he was coming down. The day seemed a lot brighter after he had seen the black and yellow jumper lying on its side hissing, and Dave crossly brushing the creepy-crawlies out of his hair.

Quite sharply they came out of the green-blue cloud shadow into the bright sunlight and here, where some bushes were clustered in a damp valley bottom, they all got off to enjoy the sunshine and hunt for new plants.

Sanchez had already caught a fine specimen of the hunting lily, a little plant that rushes about catching spiders, when Tanya came over to see him and Mike.

"Now what do you think of the Empty Planet?" she asked. "Isn't it just as weird and wonderful as we told you?"

"Oh, it's all right," said Sanchez, who was a little hurt because Tanya had gone off with Dave Anderson when they arrived. "But we see so many new worlds in *Dragonfall 5* that it takes a lot to surprise me!"

"Wait till you see a moving forest," said Tanya. "That will shake you!"

"I don't know about that," said Sanchez, still playing things cool. "I remember once when we landed on—Oh! ouch! What is it? Oh my suffering trousers! Help me!"

And he leaped up from the ground where they had been sitting and jumped about with the most agonized expression on his face, his hands clutching at the seat of his jeans.

"Stand still a minute!" ordered Mike, who had jumped up with him. Most of the students had turned to see what was causing Sanchez's wild shouts, and Miss Leas was hurrying over.

"I bet I know what it is," said Mike, seizing hold of Sanchez. "I bet it's a—Yes! Here it is!" He bent down and pulled off a small creeping plant that had a firm hold of Sanchez's jeans. There was a sharp ripping sound, and another

shout from Sanchez as Mike pulled the plant away.

"It's a scissor-wort," exclaimed Tanya. "Poor you!" and a loud shout of laughter went up from everyone within earshot.

"What's a scissor-wort?" asked Sanchez, peering angrily at the plant in Mike's hands.

"Quite rare, fortunately," laughed Miss Leas, who also taught botany, as she came up and popped the plant into her collecting cage. "It wriggles about in the turf and feeds by snipping bits off bigger plants with the jagged edges of two of its own leaves. See! It's trying to scissor through the wire of the cage now."

Everyone gathered to look at the fierce little green plant scraping busily away at its prison walls.

"Look what it's done to the seat of Sanchez's jeans!" called Dave happily.

Sanchez swung around quickly, but not before everyone had seen the big ragged cut in the blue material, with quite a piece of Sanchez showing through. He blushed furiously as everyone laughed again.

"I hope it hasn't cut you as well as the cloth, has it?" asked Miss Leas, trying not to smile.

"No, Miss Leas," said Sanchez firmly, backing away from them. "I'm quite all right, thank

46

you!" and he vaulted neatly onto the seat of his jet jumper, resolving to sit there for the rest of the field trip.

"All right, everybody!" said Mr. Radmunzen, the science teacher, coming up just at the right time to save Sanchez from too much teasing. "Next stop, Lost Wood Hollow. I want us to get there by three o'clock. We have a lot to see. A chocolate bar for the first person to get to the top of Round Beacon Hill!"

With a sputter of "blops" and "plomps" the jet jumpers got under way again, pounding off up the hill, leaving round circles of torn grass. Sanchez drove very carefully at the rear. He was not going to risk a spill with a hole that size in his pants.

When he bounced up to the top of Round Beacon most of the others were there already, and of course it would be Dave Anderson who had gotten there first and was noisily eating the promised chocolate bar. But Sanchez immediately forgot this as he looked down into Lost Wood Hollow.

"Those are the Stones," said Tanya, who had come up nervously beside him and was waiting to see if he was bad-tempered.

"The Stones!" said Sanchez, almost in a whisper. "But they're beautiful!"

Below them was a wide hollow, perfectly round as though it had been dug out, about half a mile across at the center. Down at the bottom in a great half circle, some only six feet high, some as much as fifty feet, were the Stones, poised, balanced, almost alive, springing straight from the deep green turf.

The jumpers were still; it was silent again. The afternoon sun slanting down into the hollow cast dark writhing shadows behind the Stones, all loops and bars and whorls.

"I'm sorry," said Sanchez to Tanya. "The Empty Planet is twice as weird and wonderful as you ever said it was. I deserved to be nipped by the scissor-wort plant." She smiled at him happily.

"I think they were people once," she said, "and they were dancing there when they got turned to stone."

"They look like musical instruments to me," said Sanchez. "Do you see what a lot of them are thin shapes bent over fat shapes as if they were going to strike notes on them?"

"And nobody knows," said Mike solemnly, "what they are, or who made them, or how long they've been here. They just wait for the world to end."

"First to the bottom gets two bottles of soda pop!" called out Dave, spoiling all the atmosphere of the place.

"I didn't say so!" said Mr. Radmunzen, cross at the broken stillness. But it was too late. All of them were up in their seats again, fingers pressing jet buttons. "Plomp," "blop," the jet jumpers were away down into the hollow with a chorus of hunting cries and cowboy calls, transistor radios playing away.

The field trip group settled down for refreshments right in the center of the half circle of Stones. Gray, twisted, threatening, beautiful, the Stones seemed always just about to reveal what they were for but never quite came to it. Mr. Radmunzen gave the students a brief talk on these Stones and on the Stones in other sites on the Empty Planet.

"We should be very proud to have these Stones," he finished, smiling over at Sanchez. "They are so famous that museums everywhere in the universe are asking for specimens to study, and the parents of our young friend Sanchez are taking some to Arkel X at this very moment."

"Well let's hope," said Dave in a low voice so that Mr. Radmunzen could not hear, "that they can steer their old starship better than their son steers his jumper, or they won't get very far."

With everyone starting to get out their snacks not many people heard this remark, but Sanchez did. He was very angry, and he could not start a fight in front of everybody but he had to do something.

"Where are these walking trees?" he asked Mike. "Couldn't we go to see some while the rest are feeding their faces?"

"I know how you feel," said Mike. "But don't let him see that he's got your goat. Let's eat quickly and then go. I'm sure I saw a grove of trees down in the next valley when we were on top of Round Beacon Hill. It won't take us a minute on the jumpers."

So they quickly ate their way through the dried fruits and nuts, the fresh fruit fudge, and the extra-fizzy tingle pop. It was growing darker in the Hollow now, as the sun had gone behind the hydrogen ice cloud, where it shone in dull rainbows of color. People began to sing, as they usually do toward the end of an excursion, first *I'll Go No More Aroving*, and then *Green Grow the Rushes Oh!*

"This one takes ages to sing," said Sanchez. "Let's go quickly now." So they slipped off to the jumpers, mounted their two craft, and hopped quickly over the hill.

"One is one and all alone,
And ever more shall be so."

sang the other students among the Stones, and no one noticed the two boys going.

There was a curious electric feeling in the air as they drove down into the next valley.

"If there were any black clouds about, I'd say it was going to thunder," called Sanchez.

"There never are any clouds here except ice clouds," Mike shouted back, "and there's never a wind. Thunder just happens without warning. There! you're right."

A crackle of low, threatening thunder sounded about them and pale blue lightning shimmered in a curtain. They drove around a fold in the hill.

"Look, the trees!" Sanchez cried.

There, as they rounded a corner in the valley, were the walking trees, lit by dim lightning in the darkening evening. As they got to within a few yards of the grove the boys stopped their noisy jumpers and got off. Sanchez even forgot the rip in his jeans.

The trees, about thirty of them, were halfway between a poplar and an elm in shape. Most

51

were fully grown but there were four or five baby ones near some tall ones, touching them as if they held their hands. All their roots were exposed because, as the boys drove up, the trees had been moving slowly and deliberately down the valley. But now they stood still, waiting in an eerie hush.

"Don't they like us?" asked Sanchez. "Why have they stopped?"

"Listen," said Mike sharply, cocking his head. "Can you hear something?"

The lightning still hissed in the upper air and there was the mild crackle of thunder, but above that, over the hill where they had just come from, a strange slow music like great bells and gongs sounded.

"Whatever is it?" asked Sanchez. "Look! The trees have heard it—that's why they stopped."

It was true. As the heavy haunted notes came from Lost Wood Hollow, the trees all seemed to shiver and rustle excitedly to one another for a moment. Then they were calm again, listening.

"It must be coming from the Stones," said Mike. "I don't like this. It's never happened before—and look, the lightning seems to be more intense just over the Hollow."

"This music seems to shake somewhere inside you," said Sanchez, "but it's beginning to go away. I'm glad. My head aches already."

"Let's get back to the others," said Mike. "You've seen your walking trees."

"Yes, right," Sanchez replied. "But look, they've started walking again, only now they're going up the hill toward the Stones!"

"Come on!" Mike sounded worried, but as the two boys drove sideways back up the hill the deep bell notes died quite away and the dancing blue lightning faded into a rare flicker. Behind them, very gradually, in a complicated reaching out of the roots, the trees also climbed the hill. Their roots rattled a little and their leaves fluttered gently.

Mike got to the top yards ahead of Sanchez, whose jet jumper kept slipping as he hit the steep slopes. Mike just sat where he was, looking down into the gathering darkness.

"What is it, Mike? Is everything all right?" Sanchez blurted out anxiously. Mike turned a white face to him.

"They've gone!" he said. "They've completely vanished!"

Desperately fast, recklessly rushing the worst slopes, the two friends drove down to the Stones and leaped off their jumpers.

Where they had left their party was a litter of picnic boxes and a few transistor sets, now silent. The jumpers of the field trip were parked about fifty yards away. But of children and teachers there was no sign. Only the smooth tangled surfaces of the Stones loomed up in a tense silence.

As the boys looked frantically behind the great shapes, hoping that perhaps it was all a joke, the rim of the hollow became dark with more shapes. The walking trees had reached the top and now stood grouped, watching and waiting against the yellow sky. Night was falling on the Empty Planet.

4. The Walking Trees Talk

An hour later the bells were trilling in Harvey Allen School for the beginning of evening lessons. Children were hurrying up and down the corridors, teachers were setting up their equipment, and a few last greedy people were gobbling an extra helping of supper in the dining room. The principal was in his office looking grumpily out at the darkened garden, thinking what he was going to say to Mr. Radmunzen for keeping the field trip out so late.

"Work is work," he was saying to himself, "and play is play, and I like the two kept clearly separate."

"Bang! Bang! BANG!" came thundering at his door, and before he could turn to say "Come in," a dirty, oil-smeared boy with wide, frightened eyes and a big rip in his jeans had burst into the room and was sputtering words out. It was Sanchez. He had just driven back through the night by himself with three nasty spills from his jumper.

"They've all gone!" he said hopelessly. "We searched and searched, but they've all gone! The lot of them!"

"Sanchez!" said the principal very firmly,

"you will sit down here," he swept up a chair, "and you will control yourself until you can speak and make sense."

Sanchez did as he was told and tried to relax in his chair.

"Now," said the principal, "tell me just what has happened."

Very carefully and exactly, leaving nothing out, Sanchez told how he and Mike had gone to see the walking trees, had heard the strange music, and had come back to find that everyone else had vanished.

"And you say that the jet jumpers are still there?" questioned the principal, beginning now to look very worried.

"Yes," said Sanchez, "and Mike said that he would stay there while I came to tell you. In case the music sounded again and everyone came back."

"Very sensible!" said the principal. "Wait here." He hurried out of the room much more quickly than you would think anyone so fat could move.

In five minutes he had organized a search party of twenty teachers and older boys, including Tim, who had lost at jet polo and was angry at having missed everything. Sanchez told them all over again what had happened.

"But I don't think it will do any good searching again," he ended gloomily. "Mike and I looked everywhere and there weren't many places to look. Please will you get my mother and father on the visi-phone? They don't leave in *Dragonfall 5* until tomorrow. Ask them to bring Jerk here. He's my Flying Hound Dog and, though he can't fly, he is a tremendous tracker. And *Dragonfall* might be useful too, for aerial views."

"More good sense!" said the principal. "Will you see to that immediately, Miss Matlow?" he asked the assistant principal, who was looking very upset but not being very helpful. "And now into the anti-grav bus and back to Lost Wood Hollow! Fast!"

The anti-grav bus was like a low-flying jet airplane without wings, and was much faster than a jet jumper. The moon was up now and its light, falling through the ice cloud, was broken into cold colors. The smooth hills shot past them and in minutes they were circling about the Stones. Down below, Mike's lonely figure was waving to them.

He had little new to tell them. The walking trees had gone back out of sight, the transistor radios still would not work, and there had been a little more thunder and lightning. The principal organized everyone into two's, putting Mike

58

and Sanchez together, and sent them off on jumpers to search all the surrounding hills.

"Shine your headlights all the time," he ordered, "and stop every two minutes to call and listen. If you find nothing come back here in one hour. I shall remain here to examine these Stones for clues."

Soon all the search parties were away, leaving the principal and his flashlight, a solitary light in the dark hollow.

The lightning was coming nearer again, crackling wickedly in the sky and sometimes running along the ground. It made it very easy to pick their route, and Mike and Sanchez were soon quartering the ground in the next valley. A little way ahead of them was the same grove of trees that they had met before, but now their roots were in the ground, and they were clustered tightly together as if for protection.

"They don't like this lightning," explained Mike.

"I don't like it either," said Sanchez. "Every now and then my hair goes on end with electricity. But why do you suppose those trees followed us up the hill to look at the Stones? They must have known something odd was going on. Could they have built the Stones?"

"They're very old," said Mike, "but no one

ever sees them using any tools or doing anything except walk about. They seem to talk to each other but no one's ever understood anything they say."

"Has anyone tried to get any Minims to telepath to them?" asked Sanchez, fiddling about in his knapsack.

"Yes, lots of times," said Mike, "but the Minims say they just get blocked out. The trees won't let them listen to their thoughts."

"I went up to my room while the principal was getting the search party together," said Sanchez, "and picked up our Minims. See, here they are." He fished them out of his knapsack. "I thought I'd try them on the trees, because if anything can tell us where Tanya and the others are it's the trees."

The Minims sat on his shoulder preening their fur and peering about with their beady black eyes.

"This lightning won't help," said Mike. "Stars and stalactites! Look at that!"

A sudden bright flash of lightning had struck in the center of the trees ahead of them, flaming about the branches which shook and turned as if in pain. Thunder split the air about them.

"That little one's on fire," shouted Sanchez.

"Look at the flames on that one branch! Come on, let's beat it out or it'll all go up!"

The two boys pelted along to the little tree on the edge of the grove. One of its branches was sparking and burning after the lightning bolt. A deep rustling and creaking stirred all the other trees.

"Give me a leg up," cried Sanchez, and Mike shot him up into the little tree. There, for a flurried minute, Sanchez beat and battered at the creeping flames with his coat.

"There and there!" he flailed away at the smoldering bark, "that's the end of that." He jumped down and looked up at the waving branches of the bigger trees.

"Hard luck for the little tree," said Mike, "but good luck for us. If they're not grateful now, then they ought to be! Let's take your Minims to that big tree in the middle and try them out. Minims, you must do your best! Tell them that it's my sister. Telepath to them like fury."

The Minims chittered away to each other in their own language for a minute and then replied. They always split their speeches up into three parts to give everyone a fair turn.

"We will do our best, but—" said the first.

"This is a hard task which—" said the second.

"You set us—" ended the third.

An intense silence settled on the grove. In the distance you could hear the "plomp! plomp!" of other searchers on their jumpers, but the branches no longer stirred and the leaves did not rustle in the windless air.

The three Minims had shut their little eyes tightly and their minds were reaching out telepathically trying to pick up the thoughts of the trees—if there were any to pick up. Mike and Sanchez hardly dared to breathe. Minutes passed.

Then, just as Mike was going to burst out with some remark, the tall tree near which they stood creaked deeply once, twice, and a rippling stir ran through all its branches.

Immediately the three Minims began the most extraordinary performance. They croaked and strained in their pouchy little throats until their eyes nearly popped out, and they puffed and hissed and blew between their lips into their furry paws making the nearest they could to leaf noises.

"They're getting through!" whispered Sanchez. "The trees are talking to them!" But Mike nudged him quiet and the trees and the Minims creaked and rustled away to each other for minutes. At last there was a pause. The Minims looked very tired.

"Will they speak to us, Minims?" asked Sanchez.

"Yes," piped the first Minim, "but—"

"They will not—" said the second.

"Answer questions—" finished the third.

"Why ever not?" asked Mike angrily.

"They say—" said the first,

"And we are sorry about this—" added the second,

"That you are not clever enough," said the third, and the three Minims did a little nervous giggle together.

"Well I like that!" exclaimed Sanchez. "So that's why they won't talk to people. They can put out their own fire next time!"

"Don't let's waste time," said Mike. "Get them talking about the Stones, please, Minims."

"Right," said the first, "but it will take much tiring effort."

"So—" said the second, who was the smallest and was never given much to say.

"Shut up!" finished the third, who was their leader.

So Sanchez and Mike sat down on the ground and, for the next half hour, while the thunder

grumbled and the moonlight winked changing colors through the ice cloud, the walking trees talked to the Minims. Sometimes the Minims creaked and rustled back, as if they were clearing up a point, but never for long. The boys almost went to sleep with all these lulling tree sounds. At last it ended.

"Now what have they said?" asked Mike eagerly. "Anything about Tanya?"

"They're going!" cried Sanchez. "Hi! tell them to stop! We haven't finished with them."

"Trees—"

"Never—"

"Stop," said the Minims.

"They—"

"Please—"

"Themselves."

It was quite true. With a great grumbling and tearing of earth, all the trees were lifting their roots out of the ground, showering the boys with soil. When they were raised up on their roots the biggest tree of all gave a deep creak, and they all set off down the valley.

Sanchez was carefully brushing the dirt off the Minims' fur and telling them how good and useful they were, since if you do not do this often they sulk.

"Now," he said, when he had gotten them tidy and clean, "what did they say?"

"It's a long story," said the first.

"So—" said the second,

"You might as well sit down again," said the third.

The two boys did as they were told and this is what they heard.

"Long, long ago," began the first Minim, "the Empty Planet was ruled by the Great Ones. They were a people who had all knowledge and all happiness, but they were very bored. Life wearied them."

"This," said the second, speaking very fast so as not to be stopped, "was because they lived forever and they could not die."

"Gosh!" said Sanchez. "Immortals!"

"So," went on the third Minim, "they built the Stones, and every thousand years when they were very bored they would come in a great crowd to the Stones, with all their friends to say goodbye to them. And there, after much singing and music, the Stones would begin to play, and all who sat within their circle would go by electric transport of matter to the Caves of Ice to sleep for a thousand years."

"Did they never come back?" asked Mike.

"Yes," continued the first, "after a thousand years their friends would go to the Stones again to make a sad noise and call their number, and they would return from the Caves of Ice."

"But soon—" squeaked the youngest.

"They grew bored again," butted in the leader, "and in the end all the Great Ones left for the Caves of Ice where perhaps they sleep forever. We do not know. For many many years we have not heard the Stones make music. Not until this evening when we heard the music again. We went to look and we believe that your friends have gone also to sleep in the Caves of Ice. Perhaps they were bored."

"They certainly weren't bored!" said Mike.

"It was just a dreadful mistake," said Sanchez. "You know how they were all singing *Green Grow the Rushes Oh!* when we slipped off? That must have started up that darned mechanism again, the electric transport of matter, and they've all gone by mistake to the Caves of Ice." He shivered.

"But where are the Caves of Ice?" demanded Mike frantically. "We've got to get there fast."

"We—"

"Asked—"

"That," chanted the Minims.

"The answer was hard to believe," said the first doubtfully.

"The trees told us that the Caves of Ice—" said the second.

"Were in the moon!" said the third Minim unhappily.

"In the moon!" gasped the two boys together.

"But no one ever goes there," said Mike. "It's very dangerous, and almost impossible to land on."

The Minims were silent. They never had ideas of their own; they were just good at telepathy. The boys sat looking gloomily up at the night sky.

"Is it possible to send people from one place to another by electricity?" asked Mike.

"Some people think so," Sanchez told him, "but nobody has been able to manage it yet. Old Elias says that when they do, it will be the end of starships because no one will need them. These Great Ones must have been very clever."

"It didn't do them much good if they were bored stiff," said Mike sensibly. "Poor Tanya. The Empty Planet's moon is one hundred and fifty thousand miles away!"

"Has it got only one moon?" asked Sanchez getting to his feet. "There seems to be another light coming up over the horizon."

Mike got up and the two watched puzzled as a second light began to glow over to the west. Nearer and brighter it came, and with it a low thundering noise that also grew.

"It's *Dragonfall 5!*" shouted Sanchez, leaping with pleasure. "Big Mother and Old Elias are coming back. Now we'll be all right!"

The light in the sky split into two and soon *Dragonfall 5* was swooping over their heads, a dark, slim shape between her two rocket pods that spouted flame. Old Elias was not trimming very well but perhaps he was in a hurry. The starship bore down over the hill into Lost Wood Hollow. They heard the thrum of her anti-grav tops spinning, and then silence as she landed.

"Let's get back and tell them what we've found out," said Sanchez. For now that *Dragonfall* was back he knew there would be some action.

"If there's any truth in it," said Mike wretchedly. "It all sounds very unlikely to me."

When they arrived they found Big Mother and Old Elias talking very seriously to the principal. Only Jerk made a fuss over Sanchez when he saw him. Most of the search party had returned but no one had found any sign of the missing students. Tim had tried out his miniature radar but had only detected some moving bushes.

"Actually we've got quite a lot to tell you," said Sanchez.

"But it may be all nonsense," said Mike.

"Let's all sit down in the school bus," said the principal, "and you can tell us." So they did, and told every last word that the trees had said. When they had finished everyone looked at everyone else.

"That really is very puzzling," said the principal. "It is the first time that the trees of the Empty Planet have ever spoken to anyone. I don't know what to think. Twenty years ago the starship *Thunder Dawn 3* tried to land on the Empty Planet's moon. It crashed, I'm sorry to say, and several of the crew were badly hurt. No one has ever tried to go there since."

"Well, we're off there tomorrow!" declared Old Elias very firmly. "In *Dragonfall 5*."

"Tomorrow?" said the principal, and everyone looked very impressed but too tired to say much.

"And now," cut in Big Mother, in her usual definite way, "you can all go to bed!"

The principal looked at Big Mother for a moment, two firm fat people face to face.

"Madam," he said, "you are absolutely right!"

"My boys can stay here in *Dragonfall 5*," went on Big Mother. "I reckon we'll be making an early morning start. Don't want the grass growing under our feet."

"How true," said Old Elias.

"So I'll say good night to you gentlemen," added Big Mother and got up.

"I can stay with you, can't I, and go to the moon?" Mike asked very earnestly.

Big Mother looked at the principal. After a pause he nodded slowly.

"Just so long as you don't mind sleeping with the dog," said Big Mother, getting out of the school bus.

So the evening ended with a laugh, which was more than you might have expected, but with Big Mother around nothing ever seemed too serious.

5. The Caves of Ice

Mike woke up next morning in the hammock they had hung for him from the cabin roof. It was very early. Only a faint gray light came through the cabin windows, and he would never have awakened of his own accord had his hammock not been next to Jerk's so that Jerk's big long silky tail kept brushing Mike's nose.

Jerk was sitting looking down from his hammock, and when Mike looked down too he saw that everyone else was up and quietly getting ready for blast-off.

Old Elias was somewhere at the back tinkering with the star drive, while Tim and Sanchez were checking the rockets and preparing the circuits for the countdown. Big Mother was frying corn fritters on a little stove and stirring a savory applesauce.

"Breakfast!" she said, seeing Mike looking down at her. "And we'll be under way in fifteen minutes so hurry. There's a bowl of fresh dew outside and a bar of soap."

Mike jumped down.

"I'm in charge of blast-off today," called Sanchez, looking around proudly.

"But no one's landing us on that moon except me," said Old Elias, coming in from the back and snatching up a corn fritter.

Mike went outside into the cold damp morning. The moon, still high in the sky, looked very far off and icily dangerous. A faint glow of yellow in the east showed where the sun would rise. A few yards away the Stones stood twisted and waiting. Mike shivered.

Big Mother had said there was a bowl of fresh dew but she had not said that everyone else had washed in it already. He just dabbed the corners of his eyes and came in to munch the fritters.

"Two minutes to blast-off," called Sanchez, who was eating his breakfast strapped into the pilot's webbing.

"Fasten yourselves in, boys," ordered Big Mother, and they all did up their safety harnesses. A trembling and humming shook *Dragonfall 5* as the fuel in the rocket pods began to expand and mix itself.

"Thirty seconds!" called Sanchez, squeaky with excitement.

"Concentrate, boy, concentrate!" snapped Old Elias. Big Mother slid into her safety harness nearer to the pilot's seat. Mike felt sweat breaking out on his forehead. He had never taken off in such an old-fashioned starship before. Lots of things could go wrong.

"All systems go," said Tim quietly in the co-pilot's position.

The last ten seconds clicked noisily by. The hum turned to a roar, the roar to a thunder. *Dragonfall 5* trembled onto her tail unit and rose, like sunrise before its time, flaming out of the dark green hollow.

"Gosh," called Sanchez, "look at the trees!" and even as he turned to look at the new forest *Dragonfall's* nose faltered. Big Mother shot across the cabin with a speed you would never have expected and slammed down on the power button. With the new surge of power the old starship shuddered and recovered. The ground fell away and the crew breathed again.

"Just like his father," said Big Mother. "I grow to expect it!" She moved back to her couch, and Sanchez blushed very red.

"Did you see?" said Tim, to break the awkward silence. "A whole new lot of walking trees had come up in the night and gathered around the top of the hollow. They must be expecting action."

"Well, they'll get it," said Old Elias. "But these plaguey rockets are too slow. Out of the way, son! I'm going into star drive." He took Sanchez's place.

74

"It didn't work very well last time," Tim muttered, but Old Elias paid no attention.

Dragonfall 5 was now pointed straight for the Empty Planet's icy moon. As Old Elias fiddled at the controls the flames died in the rocket pods and the only sound was the rush of the thin air outside. Already they were doing twenty thousand miles an hour and were well above cloud level.

A sharp piercing whine began from the heavy star-drive unit in the tail. It rose until it seemed to cut Mike's forehead, then died. Outside, the view disappeared and a gray mist swirled around. The starship moved faster than light, faster than time for a few seconds.

"That ought to do it," said Old Elias, champing at his beard. He stabbed the control buttons and with a "pop" sound, like being in a bubble as it burst, *Dragonfall 5* came back into ordinary space and time.

"Should be just ahead of us," said Old Elias doubtfully.

They all peered out at the blackness of space. There was nothing in sight at all.

"In fact," said Tim in a very superior voice, "the moon is now just over one hundred thousand miles behind us!"

"Hum!" said Old Elias sharply. "Overshot a bit. Still it's saved us fifty thousand miles. Return to rocket power! Engines to eight point five power and around we go." Happily their father swung *Dragonfall 5* about in a great circle of fire. The pressure of the turn squashed everyone against the walls.

"We'll be there in under two hours," he said as he settled down to enjoy the journey. They all knew how much more he liked rocket flight than star drive. Big Mother winked at the boys and began knitting.

So in fact they had plenty of time to talk before they reached this sinister moon.

"I wonder what the trees meant," said Sanchez, "when they said that to bring people back from the Caves of Ice you made a sad noise and called their number. How did you know what their number was?"

"Probably it will be all clear when we get to these Caves of Ice," said Tim confidently. "That's where my miniature radar will come in handy. All we have to do to find the caves is to circle the moon with my radar on, and if we pass over any hollow inside the moon the bleeps on my radar will tell us. At least," he added, "that's what ought to happen."

By mid-morning *Dragonfall 5* was going into her first circle around the moon. They were all rather quiet because, now that they were close, the icy surface of the moon looked very wild and quite impossibly jagged to land on. Also strange currents tugged and pulled at the starship, and Old Elias had to fight at the controls.

"Worse than a darned horse," he grumbled.

Just three quarters of the way around, Tim's radar set suddenly turned from a "bleep" noise to a "bloop" sound, and its arrow pointed to a square green mark on the black dial.

"I bet that's it," said Mike. "Look down there! Can you see a kind of kink in the ice with four regular cracks, that must be miles long, pointing to it?"

"He's right!" said Sanchez excitedly. "That must be the cave entrance all frozen over with hydrogen ice."

"Fasten your seat belts," ordered Old Elias. "This is going to be tough!"

It was. As the old starship swung and began to back, tail first, down to the tangled ice heaps below, the currents became stronger and stronger. The whole cabin shook and Jerk whimpered sadly. Big Mother stopped knitting.

"Pesky magnetism!" muttered Old Elias, squeezing out a blast of rocket power as their tail dropped to within feet of a sharp ice peak. They zoomed noisily up again, quivering with the strain.

"No wonder that other ship crashed," said Tim. He had gone quite white. Only he and Old Elias could really see how dangerous the descent was.

"We're right over that kink in the ice!" said Sanchez screwing his head round to see. "It's nearly all heaps of ice but I think I can see some stonework behind it. Something square at any rate."

"Soon see more than that," said Old Elias, grinning. "Let's try a backfire!"

Again he stabbed the controls. The rockets seemed to choke and die. *Dragonfall 5* fell back with an unpleasant swoop like going down in a fast elevator. Then, just as its tail seemed bound to crumple on the ice, there was a terrific boom from the rockets, a backsurge of black soot, and an intense flood of flame. In seconds everything disappeared in a cloud of hydrogen steam as the ice melted in the enormous heat of *Dragonfall 5*'s backfire. Old Elias chuckled as he held the starship steady and throbbing in the mist he had created.

"Should clear the ground a bit! Always wanted to decoke those engines!"

"Won't the hydrogen burn?" asked Tim anxiously.

"Where's your science, boy?" Old Elias

snapped. "Can't burn without oxygen, can it? No oxygen here! Into your space suits now; you're going to need them."

"There are only two suits the right size," said Tim, trying to peer through the steam and vapor outside.

"Then you put one on and Mike will put on the other," decided his father.

"Oh, Old Elias!" said Sanchez in dismay.

"We might need you, boy," said Old Elias with another chuckle, "if we have a difficult takeoff!"

That shut Sanchez up. He stared gloomily through the ports while Tim and Mike got into their space suits except for the oxygen helmets. Gradually the steam settled and they could see that *Dragonfall* was poised above a gully from which all the ice had melted in the great back-fire. Just along the gully were the clear outlines of a huge open doorway carved in the rock.

Old Elias brought *Dragonfall* carefully down onto the rock floor. The thunder and tremble of the rockets died away. Above them towered the rock and ice. It was not a friendly place.

"Helmets on and out you go! Don't be long. It's no health resort," ordered Old Elias.

"Look after yourselves and find Tanya," said Big Mother.

Tim and Mike climbed out through the double doors of the air lock and scrambled down toward the doorway they had seen. It was even bigger than they had thought, pitch black inside, but over the top something was written in an unknown writing which twinkled like broken glass.

"Wonder what it says!" said Tim into the radio that linked him with Mike.

"Beware of the dog, I expect," replied Mike with a nervous laugh.

"Not far wrong," said Tim. "Look!"

Just inside the entrance was a big square block of ice. In the light of Tim's head lamp Mike could see that inside the ice, fast asleep, lay a huge creature like a lion with a narrow spiky mane more like a trimmed pony's.

"Golly!" said Mike. "Some dog!"

Behind the lion creature was a long control panel. Button after button after button glowed green, in row upon row. Each button had a squiggle in the unknown writing beside it. Only a few buttons near the entrance were dark.

Tim was very interested in all this, but Mike was more anxious to find his sister. He walked on into an enormous cave as high as a church and apparently endless.

"The ice!" he gasped. Ahead, as far as his

light could reach, was block after block of ice. Each block was as big as a small house and in its shadowy depths you could see people lying in frozen sleep, side by side. They looked very much like Earth people, but with their sneering lips and long noses they all seemed very bored, even asleep.

The two boys wandered up and down, in and out of the square maze of blocks. Not all the blocks contained the bored, sleeping people. Many of them held animals like cows and horses, or smaller animals with pleasant fur or cheeky faces that must have been pets. But all were

set deep in the ice, and a chilly silence reigned everywhere.

The trees had said, "where perhaps they sleep forever," and certainly no one looked about to wake. They did not even snore.

"We'll never find Tanya and the others here," said Mike desperately. "The ice isn't even clear, and there's no end to these passages. What are we going to do?"

"Even if we found them we couldn't melt them out safely," said Tim. "We're going about it in the wrong way. Come back to that control board. I've got an idea."

They threaded their way back between the frozen sleepers to the entrance. Here Tim looked very carefully at the rows of lighted buttons.

"Shouldn't do any harm," he said, and pressed one.

"Shameen lah!" a clear toneless voice sounded from the roof above them, making them both jump and seize each other.

"What was that?" asked Mike. "Someone is not asleep after all!"

"I'm not so sure," said Tim. "Listen again." He reached forward with his clumsy heated gloves and pressed another button some way from the first. Again the inhuman voice rang out.

"Laltren kan!"

"Now," said Tim excitedly, "I'll try the button next to the first one I pressed." He did so.

"Shameen hoh!" called the roof voice, and the echoes shivered about the huge cave.

"Now the button next to the second I pressed," and again he prodded at the control panel.

"Laltren lah!" came the voice.

"Have you got it?" asked Tim, grinning across at Mike's puzzled face inside his round plastic helmet.

"No," said Mike, "except that the voice is obviously recorded."

"Don't you see?" said Tim. "It's calling numbers, the numbers of the ice blocks! Listen, I'll press five buttons one after another."

"Laltren lah!"

"Laltren hoh!"

"Laltren mali!"

"Alikat tay!"

"Alkat kan!"

"See," said Tim triumphantly, "it's like us saying 'eighty-seven, eighty-eight, eighty-nine, ninety, ninety-one.' You get it now? I bet you the next number is Alkat lah." He pressed the next green button.

"Alkat lah!" chanted the voice.

"You're quite right," said Mike admiringly.

"But how do we find the number of Tanya's ice block, and how does it help us if we find it? Pressing these buttons hasn't melted anything, has it?"

"Of course not," said Tim, "this is only for storage purposes, like a kind of register. But if we find her number we can go back to the Stones and call it. And with any luck, back they come!"

"Yes, that's a terrific idea, Tim, but how do we know which is her button?" Mike puzzled.

"It's easy!" cried Tim, "theirs is the last button with the green light because they were the last people to come here. Here it is. I know I'm right," and he pressed the last lit button before the dark buttons.

"Argen kan!" came the voice as the boys listened intently. Three times Tim pressed the button until they had it exactly right.

"Argen kan!" they both shouted.

"And now back to the Empty Planet," said Tim, "and if I never see this place again it won't worry me. They must have been very bored to want to sleep in this refrigerator!"

Five minutes later *Dragonfall 5* left the moon in another cloud of hydrogen steam. She thrashed her way through the tugging currents and blazed back toward the Empty Planet, which shone green and friendly across one hundred and fifty thousand miles of space. This time they didn't risk star drive.

"Get on the radio, Sanchez, to your principal," said Old Elias as he settled down to enjoy the flight. "Tell him to have fifty of the noisiest youngsters in your school waiting for us at the Stones. Tell him we'll be landing at three o'clock sharp. This old girl may be slow but she's punctual. Then we'll give the Stones the sad noise they asked for. Yes sir!"

6. Jerk Makes the Sad Sound

Actually, though no one would have said so to Old Elias, it was nearly half past three when *Dragonfall 5* came in with Tim at the controls to a perfect landing in the middle of Lost Wood Hollow.

The principal, most of the staff, and a big crowd of children were waiting for them, with the school bus and thirty or more jet jumpers. Circling the top of the hollow was a thick forest of Walking Trees.

"Looks like the stadium at World Series time," snorted Old Elias.

The principal met them eagerly and Tim explained what they had discovered in the Caves of Ice.

"Hmm!" buzzed the principal thoughtfully, "I suppose anything is worth trying. How are we going to arrange it?"

"I'm going to arrange it!" said Old Elias, taking his pipe from his mouth and tucking it into his back pocket. "Just let me get somewhere to stand," and he scrambled up onto a big Stone which stood like an enormous drum in the middle of the half circle.

"Now listen to me all of you," he continued,

glaring round at the circle of children until they were quiet. He went on to explain what they were going to try and how important it was. As he spoke the light began to fade and a little crackle of thunder sounded now and again in the heavy air. Even the walking trees seemed to be listening.

"Remember," he ended, "I want you to put all you've got into this sad noise. Some of you wail. Some of you groan. Some of you scream. Let's make it really gloomy. And now, just one practice of this number we've got to call. All together after me. Argen kan."

"Argen kan," everyone roared back.

"Argen kan," echoed about the hollow. The trees rustled and the lightning flashed a little nearer.

"Now for the sad noise!" said Old Elias, standing like a conductor of an orchestra on his drum Stone.

"First," boomed the principal's voice, "I must insist that everyone stand outside the circle of the Stones. I've already lost twenty-five children and two of my staff. I don't want to lose any more!"

There was a general shuffle back as he said this. Jerk got rather worked up by all the moving and shouting so Sanchez pulled him to the side and made him sit down, panting, on the turf.

89

Old Elias remained in the center of the circle, looking very small with the great Stones towering above him.

"Now," he shouted, "after that interruption I want a really sad noise. Ready, set, go!"

The most miserable hullabaloo of screaming, moaning, and wailing broke out, and went on for several minutes. Everyone did his utmost except Big Mother, who had gone back inside *Dragonfall 5*, and Jerk, who just panted.

"All right," called Old Elias, and now the lightning flashed all about the Hollow, "that should be enough. Call the number!"

"Argen kan!" everyone roared, and "Argen kan" the echo repeated.

They waited and, though the thunder shook the air, nothing happened.

"If at first you don't succeed—" called Old Elias. "Let's have another try." And again they moaned and groaned, and again they called out "Argen kan." But though the lightning storm seemed to grow more intense and the air heavier, nothing happened; no one came back from the Caves of Ice.

"Poor Tanya," said Mike. "It's got to work!"

Four times they tried, until their voices were cracking and hoarse, and still nothing happened. Despair lay heavily upon them and night was closing in. And then:

"Yowowowowow-ow!"

A most piercing yelp cut through the silence. "Yowowowowow-owp!"

Flying Hound Dogs cannot bark, but they certainly can howl!

"It's Jerk!" called Sanchez. "One of those rotten scissor-worts has got his tail!" Sanchez bent down, tore the little green plant from Jerk's splendid tail, and threw the scissor-wort yards away.

But no one turned to him, no one looked around. That long yelp had done the trick. The electric circuits in the Stones were moving. They had heard the sad sound.

"Look out, Old Elias!" shouted Tim. A long, thin, curved stone poised above Old Elias's drum was slowly swinging down toward him. Just in time Old Elias took a flying leap and landed sprawling on the grass.

"*Doing!*" the thin stone struck the drum and a bell-like note rang out. Now whole curtains of lightning played and folded across the hollow. All the Stones were in stately motion, striking, plucking, and talking in a strange sad music that filled the air and everyone's heads.

No one seemed able to think or act as the Stones made their music. Only Sanchez, who had been soothing Jerk, kept his wits about him. With a final pat for Jerk he stood up and ran into the middle of the circle. Almost lost in shimmering electricity he called out in a high, clear voice, "Argen kan!"

Then he helped Old Elias to his feet and hurried out of the circle again.

Now a rustling like a great storm came from all the watching trees. In the middle of the lightning the shape of a large square block appeared, very dim at first, then more and more clearly.

"It's one of those ice blocks!" said Tim.

"Yes, but is it the right one?" said Mike.

With a last great *"doing!"* the Stones stopped playing. A mist rose from the gleaming block of ice that stood in the center of the circle. Before their eyes the ice collapsed and a cloud of steam rose up above it. The lightning faded.

There on the grass, only just visible in the twilight, the members of the missing field trip lay fast asleep.

Everyone gave a hoarse cheer. One of the sleeping figures stirred, rubbed his eyes, and stretched himself. It was Dave Anderson.

"Oh, planets and parsnips!" said Sanchez. "Couldn't we have managed it so that he stayed on the moon?"

Now everyone was waking up. The principal was carefully counting children, and there was a general mixup of wakers and woken.

"How did all these people get here?" Tanya was asking Mike.

"What's the principal want and why is the school bus here? And *Dragonfall 5!* Are we in trouble?"

Because, of course, none of the field trip remembered a thing. They had just fallen asleep in the middle of their song when they got to the bit about "Seven for the seven stars in the sky."

Which was just as well, though Sanchez would dearly have loved to explain to Dave

Anderson what a fix he would have been in if they hadn't had an old museum piece of a starship to rescue him with.

"Hot soup for everybody!" a well-known voice cut across the chatter. Big Mother was standing at the top of *Dragonfall*'s gangway with a steaming saucepan and a pile of bowls. The field trip, all fresh from their ice block, started eagerly toward her for their chicken soup.

"Madam," said the principal gallantly, "can I persuade you to join our teaching staff? Such foresight and good sense are just what we most need." He gave Mr. Radmunzen rather a nasty look as he said this, but not really seriously.

"Two boys are quite enough for me," replied Big Mother, and she gave Tim and Sanchez a huge wink to show them how pleased she was.

It was a very cheerful picnic. There was a great deal of talk and explanation, but this time no one risked any singing.

Gradually things returned to normal in the hollow. The walking trees, disappointed that the Great Ones were not coming back after all, pulled up their roots and shuffled away over the hill. Big Mother packed up the soup bowls and everyone sat around feeling warm and full and comfortable. Except Sanchez, that is, and he was carefully dabbing disinfectant on Jerk's tail.

95

"You're the cleverest dog in the whole universe," Sanchez said, and Jerk thumped his tail because he thought that was probably true.

Old Elias had climbed back into *Dragonfall 5* where he was tinkering with the star drive.

"Time and magnetic tides wait for no man," he called down. "We've got cargo to carry if that dog's ready for blast-off."

So Big Mother and Jerk climbed back into the cabin. The rocket pods muttered into life, the old ship trembled, and the principal and all the school waved goodbye and cheered. With a surge of flame and a big cloud of soot *Dragonfall 5* reared up and stormed noisily into the quiet heavens. Quickly she dwindled to a speck of light and soon even that was gone. Only the ash and carbon dust from her exhausts remained, settling gently upon the faces of those who had watched her takeoff.

"Those engines still need decoking," said Tim, "but just let Dave Anderson say anything about an old museum piece now!"

But Dave didn't say a word. He was feeling grateful and that's always difficult.

"And now," said the principal brightly, looking at his watch, "if we pack everything up neatly and set off promptly we will just," he smiled around at everyone, "we will just be in time for evening lessons!"